ALEX FITZGERALD,

TV Star

by Kathleen Krull
illustrated by Wendy Edelson

Troll

To Allison Rose
—K.K.

This edition published in 2003.

Text copyright © 1991 by Kathleen Krull.

Illlustrations copyright © 1998 by Troll Communications L.L.C.

Planet Reader is a trademark of Troll Communications L.L.C.

Published by Troll Communications L.L.C.

First paperback edition 1998.

Printed in Canada.

10 9 8 7 6 5 4 3

The busy butterflies in Alexandra Fitzgerald's stomach disappeared.

Her piano solo in the Ocean View School's fourth-grade Christmas play had gone *perfectly*.

Kids crowded around Alex now.

"Everyone loved you!" said Alex's best friend, Becky Garcia.

"You were the star of the show," said Caitlin Williams, another friend.

"And you were so nervous," Emily Appelbaum teased.

"Well, thanks, you guys," Alex said. Then she burst into happy giggles.

All three of her friends had been dancers in the play. Another one of the dancers, Colin Ward, came over and shook Alex's hand. "Excellent!" he said.

"Thanks, Colin," Alex said. She looked around at her friends in their red and green dance costumes. "And you guys were all great in your dance number! I loved every minute."

Becky, Caitlin, Emily, and Colin beamed.

Next to them stood Elan Kent, who usually acted jealous of Alex. Now he mumbled, "Nice work, dude." He was wearing his red T-shirt that said PARTY ANIMAL.

"Watch out, Elan—we don't want

4

Fitzgerald to get conceited," Becky said. She punched Alex lightly on the arm.

"Alex is too nice for that," Emily said loyally.

Alex's dad came over and gave her a big hug. "I'm so proud of you, Alex," he said. "I wish your mother could have seen you."

Alex's parents were divorced. Usually she lived with her mom in Chicago. But this year she was living with her dad in California while her mom worked in Japan.

"I'll write Mom all about it," Alex promised. She grabbed her dad's hand and led him into the next room. Ms. Chung, the music teacher, was serving cookies and lemonade.

"A beautiful performance, Alexandra," Ms. Chung said.

Alex glowed. And now that her

stomach butterflies were gone, she was starved. She was on her fifth cookie when she heard people talking behind her.

"Here she is, Mom." Colin Ward was with his mother, who worked at a movie studio. Mrs. Ward had supplied the fake snow for the Christmas play.

Mrs. Ward stared at Alex. "You play piano so well for a nine-year-old," she said.

"Thank you," said Alex, her mouth full of cookie.

"I have a producer friend," Mrs. Ward went on. "He's looking for a little girl for a new music video. It stars Rox Rox—I'm sure you know her—that famous rock musician who started out as a child piano star?" She turned to Alex's dad and added, "Sort of like Alex here?"

Alex swallowed her cookie. She was getting very excited.

"Well, my producer friend needs someone to play the part of Rox Rox as a child," said Mrs. Ward. "Would you like to audition, Alex? All you have to do is play a simple piece and smile at the camera. I think you're just what they're looking for."

Mr. Fitzgerald turned to Alex for her answer. Alex thought about it for just a moment, then said, "Well, thanks, Mrs. Ward!"

Mrs. Ward smiled and kept on talking to Mr. Fitzgerald.

Alex went to find Becky and tell her the good news.

"Yikes, Alex—this would never have happened to you in Chicago," said Becky.

"Maybe California isn't so weird after all," agreed Alex.

"People do become TV stars here, you know!" said Becky.

Alex grinned and poked Becky's arm. "Hey—want to sleep over tonight?" she asked.

"Can't," said Becky. "Besides, you're sleeping over at my house tomorrow, remember? After we go to the movies with Emily and Caitlin?"

"Right," said Alex.

She didn't tell anyone that she had never heard of Rox Rox. Who cared? Alex Fitzgerald, star of a music video. It sounded good to her!

The next day Alex got a phone call.

"I talked to my producer friend," said Mrs. Ward. "Everything is all set. You'll audition in a few days—right after Christmas. Wear something nice, and bring along some music to play."

Alex made sure her dad could give her a ride to the audition that day. "I can't wait!" she told Mrs. Ward.

The minute she hung up the phone, it rang again.

"You ready?" Becky asked.

"Ready!"

Minutes later Becky's mom honked her horn outside Alex's apartment. Becky, Caitlin, and Emily were already in the car. Mrs. Garcia was taking everyone to the movies.

Alex's friends talked about the Christmas play. Then she told them about her call from Mrs. Ward.

"My big sister is dying of jealousy," said Caitlin. "She has all of Rox Rox's records."

Alex squirmed. She didn't want to come right out and say she didn't know who Rox Rox was. "I think I have her mixed up with someone else," she finally said. "What does she sound like again?"

The other three girls began squealing at once.

11

"Wait a minute," Caitlin said. She hummed a tune.

"No, this one." Becky sang another tune, snapping her fingers.

"Here's my favorite," said Emily. She clapped her hands while she sang. The others chimed in.

"Oh, right," Alex said. She was too polite to say that it all sounded just like a bunch of noise to her. "I'll be sure to tell Rox Rox how much you guys like her."

Emily gasped. "Do you think you'll actually talk to her, Alex?" she asked.

"No problem!" Alex said.

"Wait till my sister hears this," said Caitlin.

"Control yourself, Fitzgerald," Becky said. "I doubt you'll get to meet her. She's really a big star."

Mrs. Garcia stopped and let the girls

out. By now, Alex was so excited she could hardly pay attention to the movie. Which was a good thing, because it was a scary movie. Alex hated scary movies.

Afterward, Mrs. Garcia took them to the new ice-cream store. They ordered strawberry sundaes with marshmallow topping. On one wall of the shop, a huge TV screen showed music videos.

Suddenly Caitlin screamed. She, Emily, and Becky jumped up and down. One of Rox Rox's videos was on the screen.

Alex's mouth dropped open. This music still sounded like noise to her— not a lot different from the way her friends sang the songs.

But Rox Rox sure was beautiful. She wore high heels and tight clothes in superbright colors. Her hair was long, curly, and so blond it was almost white.

Alex liked the sunglasses the best. They had bits of glitter in them and sparkled at every note.

Alex wanted to tell everyone in the ice-cream store that soon they'd be seeing her, Alex Fitzgerald, on their TV screen, too.

"Oh, Alex," said Emily when the video was over, "you're so lucky. Rox Rox must be the most popular star in the country."

"She's even more popular in Japan," Caitlin said. "My sister says everyone's *nuts* about her there."

Alex was quiet. Just now she'd had a great idea—and she couldn't wait to get home.

On the way back, Becky poked Alex in the arm. "Don't forget you're sleeping over tonight," she whispered. "Bring your five Barbie dolls!"

"No," Alex said.

Becky drew back. "Hey, what's going on?" she said. "You don't sound like yourself."

"I'm sorry," said Alex. "I just meant I was busy tonight." She hopped out of the car. "I'll call you tomorrow."

"Sure," Becky said. She looked a little hurt.

Dear Mom,

How are you? I am fine. I am more than fine. I was the star of the Christmas play. Now I am going to be a star on TV. I am going to be in a music video with my favorite singer, Rox Rox. She is an even bigger star in Japan than she is here. Be sure to watch TV all the time. Soon you will see me playing piano. Merry Christmas.

Love,
Alexandra Fitzgerald

Alex ate another one of her dad's Christmas cookies. At least he hadn't put any mushrooms in them. He wrote books about weird and wonderful ways to lose weight. Lately he'd been on a mushroom craze.

She was so glad that Caitlin had mentioned Japan. Alex really missed her mom. Now she had a way to sort of get together with her. By becoming an international TV star.

Alex decided to write another letter, to her piano teacher back in Chicago.

Dear Mrs. Pinkowski,

How are you? I am fine.

You know how you always called me your star pupil? Well, now I am going to be a *TV* star. If you live in California, it is easy to get on TV.

I hope you will see me soon.

Your friend,
Alexandra Fitzgerald

Alex munched on another cookie. She pulled out three more pieces of paper. Then she wrote letters to her three best friends back in Chicago, telling them all about her new life in California. She thought for a minute and added:

P.S. Hope you are not having too much snow! Oh, and if you want to start an Alex Fitzgerald Fan Club, I don't mind.

Three sounded like a good start for a fan club.

The next night, Alex's dad took Alex and Becky down to the bay. Alex had heard a lot about the "Parade of Lights." Now she was getting to see it for the first time.

Many of the local boat owners had decorated their boats with multicolored Christmas lights and trim. Now they slowly paraded their boats around the bay in the moonlight. Crowds of people gathered to get a good look at how much work the boaters had done. Everyone applauded and whistled.

"There must be a million lights on some of these boats," said Alex. "This is so pretty!"

"It's kind of like fireworks, isn't it?" Becky agreed. "This is my favorite part of Christmas in California."

"Too bad I already mailed my letters— my friends in Chicago would like to hear about this," Alex said. She told Becky about all the letters she'd written to her family

and friends about her new life in TV.

Becky pointed to a boat filled with Santa, elves, and a reindeer.

Then she turned to Alex. "Hey, Fitzgerald," she said. "You didn't sleep over at my house last night because you had to write *letters*?"

"They were important—" Alex started to say.

"Don't you think you're getting a little carried away?" Becky went on. "I mean, your audition isn't for four days. And, no offense, but you haven't even passed it yet."

But Alex wasn't listening. She was having the best daydream ever. All the lights on the boats were forming into a pattern. They spelled A-L-E-X F-I-T-Z-G-E-R-A-L-D. She pictured herself playing the piano in front of a crowd of people. They whistled and applauded. Alex took a bow. . . .

Suddenly she looked around for her dad. There he was, talking to some writer friends.

She ran over and grabbed his arm. "Dad! Dad, we *have* to go to the mall tomorrow!"

"I *have* to have a new dress for the audition!" Alex panted. "Mrs. Ward said to wear something nice!"

"I'm sorry, Alex," said Mr. Fitzgerald. "The check from my publisher is overdue. I'm afraid there's no money in the budget this month for a new dress. Can't you—"

"Yikes, Dad, this is important! Please?"

"Well," he said finally, "I suppose we could make a new outfit your Christmas present this year. You won't have any packages to open on Christmas Day, though. How's that?"

"Perfect," said Alex, giving her dad a hug. To herself, she thought, *After I'm a star, every day will be Christmas Day!*

At the mall, Alex pulled her dad from store to store. She saw a department-store Santa Claus arriving by skate-board. She saw a pink store surrounded by palm trees decorated with tiny pink lights. She didn't see boots and mittens as she would have back in Chicago. Instead, people wore sandals and shorts and T-shirts, or even their bathing suits.

Hours later, she finally found just the right outfit. It was tight and brightly colored. Mr. Fitzgerald gulped when he saw how much it cost.

"It's perfect for TV," Alex said. "It's wild!"

"Well, okay," he said. "If you're sure . . ."

But then, in the next aisle, Alex saw shoes in the same bright colors. "Please, Dad?" she begged. "I don't have any shoes to match my new dress."

"Good thing you don't need matching hair," joked Mr. Fitzgerald. He pulled out his credit card.

"Hair!" Alex gasped. "I do need a haircut!"

Alex's dad sighed.

He read magazines while he waited for her to get her hair cut. All he said afterward was, "That's kind of a new look for you, isn't it?"

Alex tossed her wild curly hair in the breeze. One more thing, and her new look would be complete. . . .

Two stores down, she found it: a pair

of sunglasses with sparkly glitter in them. They weren't *exactly* like Rox Rox's, but close enough. They weren't too expensive, either.

On their way out to the parking lot, Alex stopped short. She saw just one last thing she *had* to have: a beautiful silver butterfly ring.

"I'll pay back every penny out of my allowance," she promised her dad. "But I . . . I need this for my lucky charm. So I won't get butterflies in my stomach at the audition. With a butterfly on my finger, I can't get nervous!"

As he paid for the ring, Alex thought to herself, *And this will make my hands look even better on screen.*

Mr. Fitzgerald was a bit green as he led her firmly out to the parking lot. "I hope you realize you've just received your Christmas and birthday presents

for the next several years," he said.

"Thanks, Dad," said Alex. She didn't care about holidays and birthdays right now. Making a great impression was a lot more important.

The phone was ringing when they got back to the apartment. It was Emily.

"Hi, I'm just checking to see what you're bringing to my barbecue tomorrow," she said. "You haven't told me yet."

Alex was embarrassed. How could she have forgotten all about Emily's barbecue? It was only the biggest party of the year. "Yikes, I'm sorry," she said. "I've just been so busy. I haven't had time to get anything."

"Well, then just bring yourself," Emily said politely.

"Sounds good!" said Alex. "I know— I'll bring my new sunglasses!"

"Hi, everyone!" Alex said.

Emily was having the whole fourth-grade class over for a holiday barbecue. She lived in a little house right on the beach. Her parents kept a bonfire going. They were cooking hamburgers and hot dogs, and some kids were roasting marshmallows.

Everyone said "hi" back. No one said anything about Alex's new haircut, except Becky.

"Wow, Fitzgerald, what did you do to your hair?" she asked.

Alex shook her curls the way she had seen people on TV do. "Do you really like it?"

"Come sit by me, Alex," said Emily. "Would you like a hamburger or a hot dog?"

"Oh, no, thanks!" Alex said. "I'll just have some of these carrot sticks. Being on camera makes a person look ten pounds heavier, you know. So I have to be careful—I don't want to look fat on TV!"

Alex watched kids playing tag on the beach. She ate about fifteen carrots.

"It sure is bright out here," she said to Caitlin. "I think I'll put on my new sunglasses."

Caitlin jumped up to join the tag game. Alex took her glittery glasses out of her pocket and put them on.

"Nice shades," came a voice from over by the water. It was Elan Kent. He wore a super bright T-shirt. It said ROX ROX ROCKS.

"Nice shirt!" called Alex. "I didn't know you were a fan of Rox—"

"I mean, nice shades if you're from outer space!" said Elan. He laughed a mean laugh.

"I think Martians wear glasses like that," said Colin Ward.

They took turns teasing Alex. She tried to look mad, but actually she didn't mind. She knew they were secretly impressed. They just didn't want to admit it.

Emily passed by and offered Alex some red and green ice cream.

"I'm still dieting!" said Alex with a giggle. "But, hey, Emily—since I didn't bring anything to the party, would you like me to play piano?"

Emily looked a little startled. "Well, we were just about to start a volleyball game," she said. "I wanted you for my team."

Alex knew that playing volleyball would only mess up her hair. "This would be more fun," she said. "I could play Christmas carols for everyone."

"Sure, help yourself," Emily said. She pointed to the piano in the living room.

Alex went inside and started to play "Jingle Bells."

A few kids came in to sing along. Alex heard shouts from a fast game of volleyball going on outside. She played louder, all the Christmas songs she could remember.

"I'm Dreaming of a White Christmas" was her special favorite. She thought of the white Christmas her friends back in Chicago were having. They were playing in the snow . . . coming inside to have hot chocolate . . . turning on the TV. . . .

And seeing her—*Alex Fitzgerald*—playing piano with Rox Rox!

Alex smiled dreamily.

"What song do you guys want to hear next?" she asked. Then she looked around the room.

It was empty. Alex heard kids singing "Rudolph, the Red-Nosed Reindeer." She got up and went to the window. The volleyball game was over now. Everyone was gathered around the bonfire, singing and joking around.

Everyone except Alex.

Alex leaped out of bed. Or rather, the futon in her dad's office, which was where she slept. She ran into the living room to check her dad's Christmas tree.

"Merry Christmas," she called to her dad.

Then she remembered—she wasn't getting any presents today. All the stuff her dad had bought at the mall had been her presents. No problem, Alex told herself. After all, Christmas wasn't going to make her a star. Tomorrow's audition was.

But there was a present under the tree. It was a package from Japan. Her mom had sent a box full of little toys. There was a pen that attached with magnets to a cute doll, and all sorts of other funny things to unwrap.

Her dad came into the room, yawning. "Merry Christmas!" he said. "What did Santa bring me this year?"

Alex turned beet red. "Yikes! I forgot to get you a present," she said. "I've been so caught up in getting ready for tomorrow and all. I'm really sorry—"

"That's okay," said her dad. He looked a little disappointed. "Just having you here is present enough for me. Want to help make a special Christmas breakfast? I'm cooking mushroom and avocado quiche."

"Sure, Dad," Alex said, even though she wasn't very hungry. It felt like she had butterflies in her stomach again. Probably from thinking about the audition.

She fetched her butterfly ring and ate breakfast wearing it.

The rest of the day passed slowly. In the afternoon, Mr. Fitzgerald went into his office to finish a chapter of his new book. He was taking the next morning off from writing to drive Alex to and from the audition. So he had to catch up, even though it was Christmas.

Alex practiced piano for a while. She tried on her new dress. She combed her hair in different ways. Then she decided to call up Becky.

"Hi! Do you want to come over and go for a swim?" she asked. Alex's apartment building, Palm Tree Heaven, had a nice outdoor pool.

"Can't," said Becky. "Thousands of relatives are in our house. My mom would kill me if I left." She didn't say anything about Alex coming over there.

"Okay, maybe later this week?" Alex said.

"Well, I'm pretty busy with family stuff," Becky said. "I'll see you back in school when Christmas vacation is over, for sure. But, hey! Good luck in that audition. It's tomorrow, right?"

"Right," Alex bubbled. "And I promise to get Rox Rox's autograph for you. It can be a sort of Christmas present." She knew Becky was too shy to come out and ask for the autograph.

"Well, thanks," Becky said. "But don't get your hopes up. I'll be pretty surprised if you actually get to meet Rox Rox."

"You'll see," said Alex. "Bye!"

She hung up the phone and then called Emily.

"A swim sounds fun," Emily said. "But I can't make it. We're still cleaning up

from the big barbecue yesterday. I'll see you when we get back to school!"

Alex tried Caitlin.

"Sorry," said Caitlin. "We were just leaving for church. See you around!"

They both wished her good luck in the audition.

So Alex hung out by the pool by herself and worked on her tan. Stars always had great tans.

She tried not to feel lonely. Too bad— she thought being a TV star meant having lots of friends around, but that part wasn't working out so great.

She wondered if maybe her friends were avoiding her for some reason. Maybe they were just jealous of her. Or maybe they were waiting for her to actually pass the audition.

That was it! It was just a matter of time. After tomorrow, everyone would like her again!

Alex's head whirled. She had never heard so many nice things in her whole life.

"She's perfect!" said the producer. His name was Kevin.

"She does play well for her age," said the director. Her name was Trixie. "Fitz baby, you're a lifesaver!"

Usually Alex hated to be called "Fitz." She really hated to be called "baby." But today, under the bright lights, everything seemed just right. It was like a dream come true.

"Your outfit is certainly, um, colorful!" said the woman putting on makeup. "And your hair—too much!"

"You have lovely hands, dollface!" said the man behind the camera. "Just take off those sunglasses, will you, dear?"

Glowing all over, Alex played her music one last time.

And she wasn't the least bit surprised when Kevin announced that she had passed the audition.

"Everyone, take a break for lunch," he called.

He came over to talk to Alex and her dad. "Here's the scene," he said. "This video is supposed to be on TV in two weeks. As long as you're here, we'd like to do the actual taping today. Can you stick around?"

"Fine with us," Mr. Fitzgerald said. "This way, I won't have to take another day off from my work."

"Excuse me," said Alex. "When do I get to meet Rox Rox?"

"It's your lucky day, kid," said Kevin. "Rox Rox is stopping by the set to look at your audition tape. Go have some lunch in the cafeteria. I'll send her over your way."

In the cafeteria, Alex watched her dad eat his lunch. She was far too excited for even a carrot stick.

A woman came into the room and looked around. She wore jeans and tennis shoes. She had no makeup on, and she wore plain glasses. But she had white-blond hair. Alex sat up a little straighter.

The woman came over to Alex's table. She stuck out her hand. "You must be Alex Fitzgerald," she said warmly. "Or 'Fitz baby,' as our friend Trixie would say!"

Alex shook Rox Rox's hand. "I'm pleased to meet you," she said in a high voice. "I'm one of your biggest fans."

"Hey, I'm one of *your* fans," said Rox Rox. "That was a great audition! I'm really glad you'll be in my new video." She turned to leave. "Gotta go—just wanted to say hi."

"Wait—um, could I get your auto- graph?" Alex said. "Actually, three of your autographs?" Now she could prove to Becky, Caitlin, and Emily that she *had* met Rox Rox in person.

"Sure, what did you want me to sign?" Rox Rox said.

Alex looked around. She hadn't brought any paper with her. She pulled three napkins out of the napkin holder and handed them to Rox Rox. For just a minute, she was a tiny bit disappointed that Rox Rox hadn't asked for *her* autograph.

"I love your butterfly ring," Rox Rox said as she signed the napkins. "That's the kind of ring my little sister would like. She's just about your age."

Alex couldn't believe how nice Rox Rox was. "Oh," she said politely. "Does she play piano, too, like you and me?"

Rox Rox laughed. "No, not yet! She's too busy with Barbie dolls and sleepovers at her friends' houses."

"I have five Barbies!" Alex said.

"Well, maybe you two will meet sometime," said Rox Rox. "Catch you later! Have fun at the taping—don't let Trixie get to you!" She wiggled her fingers and was gone.

Alex smiled and wiggled her fingers back. Inside she was jumping up and down. Maybe she *would* meet Rox Rox's sister. Maybe she could go on tour with Rox Rox sometime. Maybe even to Japan.

It all could happen—once she was a famous star.

Alex's face hurt from smiling so much. Her eyes burned from staring into the camera and lights. Her tight dress was making it hard to breathe. And her stomach was growling.

But she was proud of herself. Nothing kept her from acting like a total star during the taping.

The show must go on. Wasn't that what stars always said?

Perfectly on cue, she stared dreamily

into the camera. She fluttered her eye-lashes. She played the piano with a flourish, showing off her butterfly ring.

So it was very annoying when Trixie kept stopping the tape and telling her to start over.

"Fitz baby, don't take yourself so seriously!" Trixie said.

Alex was surprised. What could she be doing wrong?

She tried again.

Trixie stopped the tape after a few moments. "Please, baby, just be your-self!" she said. "Act natural."

Bit by bit, Alex stopped acting like a star. After a few more tries, she became just her regular self: a nine-year-old girl who was starting not to like being called "baby."

"It's a wrap!" Trixie yelled, satisfied at last. "Way to go, Fitz!"

Alex frowned. She was pretty sure she made a tiny mistake that time. Her only mistake all day! But did she want to run through the whole thing again? No way. So she didn't say anything.

Trixie came over as Alex and Mr. Fitzgerald were getting ready to leave. "Thanks so much," she said. "Fitz baby's part here was the last thing to be filmed. If everything goes smoothly, this video should be on the air in about two weeks."

"How will I know when it's on?" Alex asked. "So I can tell everybody to watch me?"

"We'll call you," Trixie promised. "Oh, and your check's in the mail!"

Alex couldn't wait for Christmas vacation to be over. Her friends would be so thrilled to hear about her big day at the studio!

Monday finally came, and school started up again. Music class was the first class where Alex's seat was near Caitlin, Emily, and Becky.

Alex gave them their napkins with Rox Rox's autograph. "See—I *did* meet her," she told them.

"And so you made her sign your *napkins*?" Becky asked.

"Alexandra!" came the sharp voice of Ms. Chung. "I certainly hope you're not passing notes in class. You know that's against the rules."

"No, I'm not, Ms. Chung," Alex said. She faced the front of the room and didn't look at her friends.

Ms. Chung wrote some music on the blackboard. Alex turned back to her three friends and started giggling. She whispered stories about Trixie and Rox Rox and Kevin. She laughed out loud when she told about being called "Fitz baby."

She didn't notice Ms. Chung turning around and staring at her. "Alexandra, there's no talking in class," said Ms. Chung. "I'm surprised at you!"

Alex slunk down low in her seat. But then she remembered how Rox Rox's sister liked sleepovers and Barbies. She just had to tell Becky.

Ms. Chung looked through her desk drawers for some music. Alex leaned over and started whispering.

A shadow fell across Alex's desk. It was Ms. Chung.

"Your rude behavior today leaves me no choice," she said sternly. "Alexandra, go sit in the principal's office until you think you can behave."

Alex blinked back tears. This was no way to treat a TV star!

9

Being in the principal's office was zero fun. Alex had to sit there all afternoon, too. The worst part was that by the time she got out, her friends had already gone home. There was no one for Alex to talk to.

She walked the three blocks home by herself. Yikes! Becoming a TV star was making her life in California worse, not better. She was getting in trouble at school. Hurting her dad's feelings by forgetting to buy him a present. Making him spend money he didn't have. And *losing* friends, not gaining them.

Things weren't going the way she planned at all.

Alex wasn't sure what to do. But blabbing about the video just seemed to make everyone not like her.

Alex promised herself never to talk about the video again.

Then, a week later, Mrs. Ward called up Alex. "I heard from Kevin today," she said. "The new Rox Rox video will be on TV tonight for the first time."

Alex giggled happily. Wait till she told her friends—oh, right, she was keeping things secret now.

"How would you and your dad like to come over to our house to see it with me and Colin?" Mrs. Ward went on. "Does that sound like fun?"

Alex checked with her dad. "Sounds good!" she told Mrs. Ward.

Alex wanted more than anything to stay on the phone. She wanted to call up Becky, Caitlin, and Emily, to tell everyone in the world to be sure and watch TV tonight.

But she also wanted to keep the promise she'd made to herself. So she went and did her homework until it was time to go to the Wards' house.

Alex, her father, Colin, and his mother sat around the TV, drinking cider and eating popcorn. They watched and watched.

Finally, Rox Rox burst onto the screen. She was wearing those tight, bright clothes and those glittery sunglasses.

"She doesn't look like that really," Alex told Colin.

The video was supposed to tell the story of Rox Rox's life. It was about how she started as a girl playing the piano and had grown up to be this international rock star.

Alex watched with growing delight. She tingled from head to toe.

The noisy music got quiet. Suddenly the screen showed a pretty little girl sitting in front of a piano. She wore jeans and sneakers, and she had straight blond hair.

Alex heard the same music she had played when she was at the studio. Just the way she had played it, too.

Oh, no, there was that tiny mistake she had made!

The camera zoomed in on the little girl's hands—and there was Alex's butterfly ring. It took up practically the whole screen for a second.

But the girl was not Alex. It was someone Alex had never seen before in her life.

Then the video was over.

"Um, so where was Alex?" Colin asked.

Alex was turning bright red.

Mrs. Ward left the room to make a phone call. In a minute she came back.

"Guess what!" she said. "Trixie, the director, decided at the last minute to use Rox Rox's little sister in the role of young Rox Rox. She wanted to make the most of the family resemblance."

"But that was *me* playing the notes," Alex said, getting mad.

"Right—Rox Rox's sister can't play

piano," Mrs. Ward went on. "She just pretended to play, while they used the *sound* of Alex and the shot of her hands. They really liked your hands, dear."

"But that's not fair—" Alex started to say.

"Don't worry, you'll get your check, just as promised," Mrs. Ward said. "This happens all the time in TV and movies. Please don't take it personally, Alex. It's just show business."

Alex gulped. She looked down at her hands and thought for a minute. Then she had to laugh. "Alex Fitzgerald's hands—TV stars!" she said.

"Let's give Alex a big *hand*," said Colin, and everyone clapped loudly.

On the way home, Alex turned to her dad. "I feel bad about all that money you spent on my new clothes," she said. "And then they never even got shown on TV!"

"Except for the ring," said her dad. "They got a nice shot of the ring."

Alex snapped her fingers. "I know— when I get that check from doing the video, I'll give it to you. That should pay for everything!"

"With some left over," said her dad, giving her a hug. "We can plan some special treats. Want to go see Rox Rox in concert the next time she comes to town?"

"Too noisy!" said Alex. "Let's think of something else."

As soon as Alex got home, she called up Becky.

"I'm sorry about the way I've been acting lately," Alex said. "Blabbing about myself all the time."

"No kidding," said Becky. She sounded relieved. "You know, we were all excited for you in the beginning. But, hey, Fitzgerald, you've been getting so conceited!"

"I just got carried away with the idea of being famous," Alex said.

"Everybody likes you for yourself," Becky went on. "Not because you might be a star someday. We *want* to hear your good news—"

"You do?" Alex said. So she didn't have to keep secrets?

"Of course we do," said Becky. "But can't you be a star and your own nice self at the same time?"

It reminded Alex of Trixie yelling "Just be yourself!" at her. But she didn't want to talk about Trixie right now.

"Well, my *hands* are the stars," said Alex. She told Becky all about watching the completed video that night.

"You mean, after all this, you're not

even *in* the Rox Rox video?" Becky asked, starting to howl with laughter.

Pretty soon Alex, too, was giggling so hard she couldn't talk.

That was okay. In a minute, she would get her breath back. Then they could talk about something else. Like planning their next sleepover, maybe.